Charles loved his puppy.
Her name was Cookie.

All summer long,

The First Day of School

Robin Hill School

Written by Margaret McNamara
Illustrated by Mike Gordon

Ready-to-Read
Aladdin Paperbacks
New York   London   Toronto   Sydney

For Becky & Chester and Michael & Cookie
—M. M.

🪔

ALADDIN PAPERBACKS
An imprint of Simon & Schuster Children's Publishing Division
1230 Avenue of the Americas, New York, NY 10020
Text copyright © 2005 by Simon & Schuster
Illustrations copyright © 2005 by Mike Gordon
Also available in an Aladdin library edition.
Designed by Sammy Yuen Jr.
The text of this book was set in Century School Book.
Manufactured in the United States of America
First Aladdin Paperbacks edition July 2005
20 19 18 17 16 15 14 13 12 11
Library of Congress Cataloging-in-Publication Data
McNamara, Margaret.
First day of school / Margaret McNamara ; illustrated by Mike Gordon—1st Aladdin
Paperbacks ed.
p. cm—(Ready-to-read) (Robin Hill School)
Summary: After a summer of playing with his puppy, Michael is sad to learn that she
cannot stay with him on the first day of school.
ISBN 978-0-689-86914-3 (pbk.)—ISBN 978-0-689-86915-0 (lib. bdg.)
0512 LAK
[1. First day of school—Fiction. 2. Schools—Fiction. 3. Dogs—Fiction.]
I. Gordon, Mike, ill. II. Title. III. Series.
PZ7.M232518Fg 2005 [E]—dc22 2004016672

Charles played with Cookie.

They played catch.

They played ball.

They were always together.

On the night before
the first day of school,
Charles said to Cookie,

"Tomorrow we start
first grade."

In the morning,
Charles walked to
Robin Hill School.

His mom and Cookie
came with him.

When they got to school,
Charles said to Cookie,
"Time to go to school!"

"Oh, Charles," said his mom,
"dogs are not allowed
in school."

"What?" said Charles.
"Nobody told me!"
He hugged Cookie tightly.

Mrs. Connor was the
first-grade teacher.
She saw how sad
Charles was.

"May I pet your dog?"
she asked.

"I guess," said Charles.

"He looks nice,"
said Mrs. Connor.

"She is a she,"
said Charles.
"Her name is Cookie."

"I wish Cookie
could come
to school,"
he said.

"Me too," said Mrs. Connor.
"You do?" asked Charles.

"Oh, yes,"
said Mrs. Connor.
"If Cookie came to school,
she could live
on the playground.

She could sleep
in a cubby.

She would belong
to everyone
at Robin Hill School!"

Charles gave that
some thought.
"Mom," said Charles,
"you can take Cookie
home now."

Charles had a good
first day.

But he missed Cookie.

When the day was over,
Cookie was waiting for him.

She waited for him
every day,
because she was his dog.